The
Dingle Ridge Fox
and Other Stories

The Dingle Ridge Fox
and Other Stories

Written and illustrated by
Sam Savitt

SCHOLASTIC BOOK SERVICES

NEW YORK · TORONTO · LONDON · AUCKLAND · SYDNEY · TOKYO

Copyright © 1978 by Sam Savitt. All rights reserved. This edition is published by Scholastic Book Services, a division of Scholastic Magazines, Inc., 50 West 44th Street, New York, N.Y. 10036, by arrangement with Dodd, Mead & Company.

12 11 10 9 8 7 6 5 4 3 2 1   2   9/7 0 1 2 3 4/8

Printed in the U.S.A.   15

To Bette with love

*Books by Sam Savitt available
through Scholastic Book Services:*

The Dingle Ridge Fox and Other Stories
Midnight
Vicki and the Black Horse
Wild Horse Running

Contents

The Dingle Ridge Fox

THE DINGLE RIDGE FOX was asleep on a thick mat of October leaves, nesting snugly between the spreading roots of a great maple. He slept soundly with his nose and brush tucked together, but, like other creatures of the wild, his senses were sharply alert. The distant click of a steel-shod hoof striking stone penetrated his dreams and snapped him wide awake. He rose and stretched, listening hard as his nose tested the morning breeze.

A flock of crows lifted from the floor of the valley below and soared above him, squawking loudly as they flew by. Their warning was clear—it was time to get going.

The fox had spent a long night of hunting that had taken him far from his home grounds. But in the end, he had feasted on fresh-killed rabbit and afterward had enjoyed a most refreshing nap. Actually he preferred to travel after dark, but the sharp ring of the horseshoe plus the cry of the crows meant horses—and horses at this time of year usually meant hunters and hounds.

The fox trotted off, following the ridge line so he would be able to keep an eye on the valley. He was an old pro at fox hunting, at leading the hunt a merry chase through fields and woodland, over stone walls, and through swamps. He displayed enormous confidence in his ability to outlast any horse and outrace any hound. But lately the men had seemed to outguess every strategy he used.

Earlier that month a litter mate had been killed, and just four days ago the hounds had crossed his own line up near Duhollow and run him all the way to Starr Ridge, nearly five miles away. They almost got him then. The fox had heard the hounds crashing through the brush two jumps behind, but in the nick of time he reached a highway and shot across it through a stream of traffic and squealing brakes. He reached the far side unscathed and plunged into the woods below. Behind him he could hear howling cries and the huntsman's horn desperately calling in his pack.

Now, with the memory of that chase still fresh in his mind, the Dingle Ridge fox turned toward home.

At the bottom of a narrow gully he paused for a few quick laps of water, then bounded up a steep incline to a rock ledge where he stopped to listen once more. All was silent; then suddenly a hound yelped and the unmistakable beat of horses' hoofs vibrated across the land.

As yet the fox was not sure that he was the hunted. Also, he was not about to run across strange country

14

in broad daylight if he could help it. But as he paused there, undecided, the voices of the hounds in full cry reached his ears and spurred him on up the slope. He gained the top and turned north, covering the ground at an easy lope. He was taking his time, saving his strength, for the day was young, the horses and hounds were fresh, and his den was many miles away.

Ordinarily the fox would have chosen a way that afforded the best cover, utilizing forest and wetlands to his advantage. But this was unknown territory, and the best thing to do right now was to get out of there as quickly as possible by the most direct route he could find.

The hounds came pouring up out of the gully behind him. They were really giving tongue now, for the scent was hot and their blood was up. From down below the huntsman's horn called, "Gone away, gone away!"

The huntsman came into view a moment later, mounted on a gray horse. His scarlet coat flashed in the sunlight as he galloped beside the hounds, cheering them on. In their wake the "field" appeared—a horde of riders, scarlet and black coated, leaning into the wind. Their horses were running flat out with their heads low and reaching, their hoofs ripping up huge clods of earth.

The land rolled on ahead in a series of yellowing fields separated by stone walls and rail fences. Cows looked up from their grazing to watch the fox go by. He moved straight as the flight of an arrow but veered left when he spotted a group of people standing on a high knoll to his right.

The terrain rose upward, then dipped sharply into a boulder-strewn valley of ditches and scrub growth. The fox could have circled it but he went right through the middle, running in a broken, zigzag line to slow his pursuers. A shallow brook crossed in front of him and he turned with it, bounding through the water for almost three hundred yards before he leaped up on the bank.

He stood there a moment listening, to see if he had succeeded in throwing the hounds off his trail. But all he had managed to do was slow them down. Brewster, a big black-and-tan veteran of many a hunt, seemed to pick his scent out of the air. His voice cried, "This way, this way!" Seconds later, a full chorus joined in and the pack was off and running once more.

For the next hour the fox employed every tactic he knew to shake off the hounds. He was hampered by the unfamiliar country, but as a resourceful, intelligent animal he was quick to make the most of every opportunity that presented itself. He splashed across swamps and scooted along the tops of stone walls. When he chanced upon a cowbarn, he darted right through the middle of it, to the utter surprise of a farmer standing in the hayloft, then plunged through the manure pile as he left. At one time he walked slowly in amongst a flock of sheep, careful not to alarm them, for he knew their droppings would obliterate his scent. They did, but the wily huntsman regrouped his baffled pack and cast them again where he reckoned their quarry would have come out.

As the fox cut through the back yard of a farmhouse, a pair of small terriers gave chase, yapping at his heels. He paid little attention to them, for they were accomplishing the same purpose as the sheep by mingling their scent with his.

Half a mile later, the fox happened on the track of another fox. He stayed right on it for a short while, then leaped to the top of a boulder and changed his direction, expecting the hounds to stick to the other scent.

But none of these strategies seemed to slow up the

pursuers. The huntsman knew his business. He controlled and deployed his pack with an uncanny skill that brought them closer and closer to their prey. On the banks of Titicus Lake, almost six miles south of Dingle Ridge, he pulled up to give his horse a breather. The animal's flanks were heaving and his gray coat was dark with sweat. He pranced and tossed his head, throwing huge hunks of froth back at his rider.

The master of the hunt rode up alongside the huntsman. "My horse has thrown a shoe, Jack," he announced. "I'd better pull out before he goes lame."

A good part of the field, feeling that their horses had had enough, followed the master home, but six decided to stay on to the end.

The hounds had lost the scent. They scurried along the shore of the lake, whining and yipping with anxiety. The huntsman surmised the fox had turned either right or left, using the shallow water to obscure his trail.

Suddenly somebody yelled, "Tally ho—there he goes!"

Across the lake the hunters could see the fox just making shore. They watched as he stood there for a moment, dripping wet. Then the fox shook himself and, climbing the far bank, disappeared into the heavy growth beyond.

The huntsman hurriedly gathered his hounds and sent them in a mad rush around the lake. Spray and mud flew from the horses' hoofs as they galloped along the bank to the point where the fox had vanished.

The hounds picked up the scent with a howling outcry. They scuttled through a four-rail fence and the huntsman's gray jumped it boldly, going away. The following horse chopped out the top rail and turned over, throwing his rider. The animal immediately lunged to his feet and followed the others as they went flying by. The horseless rider staggered after him shouting, "Whoa! Whoa!" But there wasn't a chance in the world that his mount would stop.

The cold swim had refreshed the tired fox. He reached the railroad tracks that pointed north and loped along them to the trestle that spanned the town sprawled out below. He slowed to a walk and crossed the long expanse, stepping gingerly on each rail tie until he made the far side.

The huntsman, far ahead of the others, sighted the fox when the animal was almost halfway over. He blew in his hounds and skirted the town, with the field of five riders and one riderless horse nearly a half mile behind.

From the beginning he had suspected their quarry was the Dingle Ridge fox but now he was certain of it. He had hunted foxes for years. He knew all about them, their habits and their strategies. But no fox he had ever known was more daring or more ingenious than this one.

By the time the hounds reached the north end of town, their prey was well on his way to Dingle Ridge.

The hunters settled into their saddles for the last lap of the race. They were bone weary, and their muscles cried out against the steady pounding. Their horses were lathered and blowing hard, and the hounds, still running on ahead with the huntsman, were tiring rapidly.

At Duhollow Junction the fox had been running for more than two hours. His red coat was all scuffed and flecked with mud and his tongue hung almost to the ground. Only his tail still managed to stay aloft like a banner, defiant to the end. He was truly close to exhaustion—but so were his pursuers.

At last he was on familiar ground. Before him spread a golf course where horsemen would not dare to follow. Beyond that between him and Dingle Ridge ran the highway.

He was moving much more slowly now, for the pace was beginning to tell. The pride in his speed had withered away and his lungs, laboring painfully, seemed grown old.

His earliest training had taught him never to leave a straight trail if a crooked one was at all possible. But under the present circumstances, a straight line was the shortest distance between himself and home. He crossed the golf course in this manner, looking neither right nor left and paying no attention to the golfers staring at him as he went by.

There was no time to look back, and he was concentrating only on that which was up front. The fox had almost reached the edge of the golf course when the hounds emerged from the woods and swept onto the green. Their cries surged through the fox like fresh blood to give him a new spurt of energy and the feeling that all was not yet lost.

The huntsman checked his horse at the edge of the velvet turf and sized up the situation instantly. The Dingle Ridge fox was leading the pack to the highway again and disaster. He circled the course at a dead gallop in an effort to head them off.

He caught up with the hounds on the far side and managed to call in most of them. But Brewster and some of the leaders had already crossed over.

The fox knew where he was going now. The closeness of his goal renewed his flagging strength. His pace picked up as he sprinted through a grove of trees and fairly flew into a rocky ravine that wound its way up a jagged slope through an impenetrable mass of windfalls and tangles of vines that would stop the horses—but not the pack.

As the hounds lunged up the draw, closing on the fox, all that could be heard was their panting breaths for they had no wind left to give tongue.

Near the top, the fox turned into the dense undergrowth. Soon in front of him a huge stone wall rose out of the gloom. It had probably been built there when the forest was a clearing over a hundred years before. But the rains and snows of countless seasons had eroded the earth on either side of it and what had started out as a four-foot wall was now almost seven feet high. The trees and vegetation pressing inward

21

had kept it from crumbling. The wall itself was impossible to scale, but several months before the fox had discovered a narrow tunnel at its base just about wide enough to accommodate him in a pinch.

The lead hound snapped his jaws on empty air as the fox dove into the shaft and frantically squirmed his way through. The hound's head followed him in but his shoulders slammed against the sides, stopping him cold. He howled with frustration and began digging madly—but the chase was over.

The fox was safe at last. He crouched against the far wall until he heard the horn calling off the hounds. Afterward he stretched out on his side with his flanks pulsating against the cool earth.

He stayed where he was for the remainder of the day, waiting for his vitality to return. Shortly after dusk he rose to his haunches. He felt sore and stiff but mostly hungry. He quenched his thirst at a nearby stream, then moved up out of the woodland.

The night was cold. An enormous orange moon climbed above the treetops to shed a soft warm light over the countryside. The fox stalked along an old cowpath to a wide grassy meadow where he knew of a hollow overgrown with coarse grass, the playground of a colony of field mice. He sat next to it and waited. Presently a faint squeak showed that the game was astir. The fox rose up on tiptoe, not crouching but as high as he could stand so as to get a better view. The runs that the mice followed were hidden under the grassy tangle and the only way to know the whereabouts of a mouse was by seeing the slight shaking of the grass and pouncing instantly upon it. The trick was to locate the mouse, seize him first, and see him afterward.

A half-dozen mice served as an adequate appetizer. Just before dawn, the fox located a white rooster asleep on top of a farmyard fencepost, and that completed his meal for the night.

As the sun came up in the east, the Dingle Ridge fox crawled into his den, well hidden beneath a rocky ledge. Inside he circled once or twice, then collapsed into a deep bed of leaves. His nose snuggled into the warmth of his luxurious tail as he slept, and as he dreamed his legs jerked spasmodically and twitched from time to time.

All the following week the fox moved restlessly through the area, mostly at night. He hunted and ate and slept but did not stray far from his home base. Sometimes he amused himself by trying to catch frogs in a pond below his den. More often he sat in the shelter of a spreading barberry bush, watching the cows graze in the valley or a redtail hawk rising and gliding against the autumn sky.

He could not help but be aware that during the past few years most of the foxes had left his part of the country and drifted toward the mountains where horses and hounds could not follow. The urge to go with them was in him, but he hung back—waiting for he knew not what.

One Saturday morning the fox turned north toward the high country. Last night a vixen had called from up there, and perhaps the time had come to move in that direction, where he would be safe.

Just as he was about to enter the forest, the long wavering notes of a hunting horn floated up to him. He turned and listened. The sound came again from the valley far below. It made his heart quicken and the blood within him sing. He crouched at the brink of a grassy ledge where he could get a better view.

He saw the hunt gathering. Instantly he picked out

the huntsman on his gray horse with the hounds milling around—whining, yelping, anxious to be on their
way. They began moving off, the huntsman and
hounds up front with the field falling in behind.

The Dingle Ridge fox rose to his haunches. He
paused there for a second, then flew down the long
slope, zigzagging his way through brush and boulders.

At the foot of the steep incline he angled across a wide meadow, running easily downgrade.

As the sound of the hunting horn echoed once more, the fox increased his pace. He knew that just ahead, and to his right, hounds were seeking a fox. If he hurried they would cross his line for another exciting race with death.

Jamie

I WAS CHECKING fence when I spotted the orange cat in the open meadow. It was coming toward me running flat out, with a huge Airedale just two jumps behind. Like a flash, the cat spun about and leaped upon his pursuer's back. The dog yelped and whirled in blurring circles, trying to dislodge his rider. Suddenly the cat was off and running once more, still heading in my direction. The befuddled dog lined him up in an instant and two seconds later was ready to close in again. The little cat repeated his maneuver of buying time astride the dog's back, then continued his race for life.

I rushed to the rescue, waving my arms and shouting like a maniac. The cat did not change course. He passed so close I could have touched him, but the Airedale detoured around me, hardly breaking his stride. He made up his lost distance in a rush but his jaws snapped the empty air as his target shot straight up a tree. The chase was over.

The little orange cat crouched on a low branch,

staring balefully at the frustrated Airedale below. After several vain assaults on the tree trunk, the dog trotted off to seek out more cooperative game.

I tried to coax the angry little creature down but he'd have no part of me. Finally I gave up and walked back to the barn to groom Belle, my black mare.

Later, as I turned to put away the grooming tools, I was startled to see the orange cat standing in the stall doorway. He sauntered in and brushed against my boot as he passed, then sat down right in front of the black mare.

Belle lowered her head to inspect the newcomer. She sniffed him all over with little blowing sounds. The orange cat was completely unruffled by this procedure. When he had had enough, he conducted his own investigation by rubbing against both sides of Belle's face, then brazenly proceeded to do the same to her legs. During all this, the horse never moved a muscle. Afterward the little cat pawed together a bed of shavings in the corner of the stall and went to sleep. He moved right in, just like that, and settled down to stay.

I named our uninvited guest Jamie. He accepted me as part of the place along with the bantams and the ducks and Little Joe, my poodle. There were two other horses in the stable, Oberon, a young bay thoroughbred, and Stagecoach, a big gray hunter. Both were kind, friendly horses but Jamie had little to do with them or the two dozen black Angus that wandered over the green pastures. Actually, the little orange cat

30

seemed to like all the creatures of High Ridge Farm, but Belle, the black mare, he loved.

The two became almost inseparable companions. When you saw the black mare, the little orange cat was not far away. Twice he stuck so close to Belle he got stepped on. The first time broke his leg, which had to be pinned for three weeks. He was no sooner mended when one of Belle's hoofs accidentally came down on his front paw, and Jamie was off to the hospital once more.

As a matter of fact, he spent a great deal of time at the vet's. His curious, adventurous spirit got him into all kinds of hassles with mowers and pitchforks and the many other pieces of equipment found around a farm.

John Werlow, the farmer down the road, figured I spent more on that cat than the little animal was worth. When the medical bills were totaled, Jamie was easily the most expensive cat in the county.

The black mare had been my favorite hunter. She was getting on in years, and I exercised her just enough to keep her old joints working. Whenever I rode her, Jamie accompanied us to the barnyard entrance and waited there, sitting atop a stone wall, until we came home.

When I turned Belle into the pasture, Jamie trotted right along behind her, his bushy tail so straight up that I could spot it a hundred yards away, moving above the tall green like a periscope.

When the horse grazed, Jamie lay on his back in front of her. As the black muzzle came close, the cat would reach up and playfully stroke the velvet lips. He was an affectionate cat, and, although he was quite small, he displayed great courage. I often saw him walk defiantly through a flock of hissing geese or casually sit in the middle of the driveway as some strange dog came stalking toward him. Jamie seemed to know instinctively if the situation called for fight or flight. And I realized then that the incident with the Airedale had not been a retreat but an orderly withdrawal.

One of his favorite games was dashing between Belle's legs as she walked into the stable from the pasture. At first I tried to discourage this sport, for I was certain he would get stepped on again. But Jamie simply could not resist the challenge of testing his speed against those steel-shod hoofs.

With autumn, the days grew shorter and colder. Now Belle spent more time in her stall and Jamie sat on her back to keep warm or lay in the hay as the black mare ate around him.

Jamie was a hunter and was forever bringing dead mice to his friend and laying them at her feet. Of course Belle did not touch them, but Jamie never got discouraged. When I cleaned the stall, I often uncovered these tokens of love and almost felt that I should ask Belle's permission before removing them.

One morning in the middle of December, I found Belle pacing restlessly around her stall. Oberon and Stagecoach were quietly munching their hay. Jamie was nowhere to be seen and it was immediately apparent to me that the black mare was disturbed by his absence. The stable was kept relatively warm by the three horses, but outdoors there was snow on the ground and it was bitterly cold. I could not imagine that Jamie would be out there voluntarily. The barn had two floors above the stable part and I made a thorough search of every nook and cranny big enough to hold a cat or a mouse.

Only two months before, Jamie had disappeared just as suddenly. But that time, I heard his plaintive meows and realized he had gotten in between the ceiling of the stable and the floor of the garage above. I finally discovered the opening he had squeezed through, and I stood there a good part of the afternoon calling his name until he was able to zero in on my voice and make good his escape.

But this day Jamie was nowhere to be found. Evening came, and feeding time. Stagecoach and Oberon gobbled their grain but Belle would not touch hers. She stood facing into the corner of her stall, terribly depressed. I took her temperature as a matter of course, but in my heart I knew what the trouble was.

The following morning when Jamie had still not come home I decided to conduct an all-out cat hunt on my own. I figured that Jamie, a dedicated mouser, would have been forced to conduct his hunting indoors out of the weather. He had evidently exhausted our stable, so what other place would do? There was an old abandoned barn a short way up the road that might fit the bill. It had been unoccupied for years and was literally falling apart.

On a hunch, I hiked up there. A high wind was relentlessly icing my forehead as I approached the creaking structure. I crouched slightly to go through the tilted doorway, then stopped long enough to blow some warmth against my cold fingers. It was semi-dark inside, moldy smelling, and completely crisscrossed by a network of dusty cobwebs. Snow had filtered in and there were small piles of it scattered over the rotted floorboards. I was encouraged when I made out a tiny cat print in one of them.

"Jamie," I shouted. "Jamie, Jamie!"

I listened for an answering meow but all I could hear was some old door banging away from above. I picked my way carefully through the debris, peering under fallen feed bins and mangers and a trembling stairway that rose to the skeletal framework of a hayloft no longer there.

I was turning to leave, disheartened, when I thought I heard a faint meow.

"Jamie," I yelled, "is that you?"

The meow came again—from below. I began frantically moving aside old timbers which had collapsed on the floor.

The meow was persistent. Now I was down on my belly squirming beneath the floorboards. I had one panicky thought of the whole place coming down around me. At last I could see two eyes staring at me out of the gloom. Evidently the little cat had been trapped by the ancient, shifting foundation. I shoved aside one last beam and there he was. I could not make

35

out his color or shape, but I knew it was Jamie. I reached in and dragged him out, then wriggled back the way I had come.

"You little son of a gun!"

I was so relieved. I held him close and ran all the way to the stable. When I witnessed the reunion of wild meows and nickers, I began to understand for the first time the depth of the devotion that existed between Jamie and the black mare.

In February, I went to Carolina for two weeks. I boarded the horses at a stable in Greenwich, Connecticut, and arranged with John Werlow to take care of the other livestock at High Ridge Farm.

When I returned home, I learned that everything had gone well. The only animal John could not account for during my absence was Jamie. His food dish had been emptied every day, but John had not seen hide nor hair of the little orange cat since I left. I went down to the barn and checked it and the surrounding area but could not locate him.

The horses came back to High Ridge Farm the following morning. As I led Belle down the ramp of the horse van, I saw a cat coming toward us across the barnyard. It was a grimy, grayish-looking creature, but something about its jaunty walk and the way it carried its head cocked to one side looked a lot like Jamie— Jamie, who was always so meticulously groomed! Yet it *had* to be Jamie! No other cat would brazenly twist itself in and around Belle's front legs as she walked— no other cat would cry so ecstatically as it cavorted on ahead, leading the way to the stall.

That evening when I went down to feed the horses, I found Jamie sitting on top of the stall door, resting against the side of Belle's face. Once again he was sparkling clean and purring with happiness. His friend had come back, and it was then I vowed that I would never separate the little orange cat and the black mare again.

Toward the end of winter, Belle began losing weight. I increased her feed but, even though she ate well, she continued to fall off. The hollows above her eyes deepened and her ribs and hip bones began to protrude.

I called Dr. Samford.

"What's ailing her, Doc?" I asked after he had examined the black mare.

The vet peered at me over his thick-lensed glasses.

"The same thing that starts ailing all of us sooner or later," he answered. "Old age."

He prescribed a tonic; however, I was convinced that the best tonic Belle could get would be the new green grass which was due soon. But the spring grass did not help. I stopped riding the old horse and tried to make her as comfortable as possible. As the summer slipped in and the days grew hot, I turned her out at night with the other horses. The air was cool and fresh then, and free of flies. Jamie stayed with her constantly, and rarely took time off to hunt. He seemed to sense that which I was reluctant to admit.

On a Saturday morning in late August, Belle failed to come in for her breakfast. I trudged to the upper pasture and saw her lying where the trees met the meadow. I knew instantly by her flatness to the earth that she was dead. Jamie sat beside her and didn't move as I came up. Our eyes met over the still form and I could feel his grief so strongly that I had to turn away.

That afternoon, I buried Belle where she lay. All the while I was bulldozing the grave, Jamie sat on an old tree stump, watching. When I finished he moved to the center of the mound of earth and stayed there. Twilight turned into night and I could no longer see him from the house.

I was unable to sleep, and a short time past midnight I went back to the pasture with a flashlight. Jamie had not moved. He was so still I could have picked him up, but somehow I felt I would be intruding.

The next morning the little orange cat was gone. I walked through the woods and fields for hours calling his name, but Jamie had vanished. I knew he would never return, for this time the black mare was not coming back.

Randy

JON RADCLIFF HAD always owned golden retrievers, and when his old dog died, he purchased another of the same breed. Although he never exhibited his dogs, he always bought the caliber of the breed that would "show." His newly acquired six-month-old puppy promised to be as handsome as any of the others.

The home the puppy was brought to was a magnificent white manor house on a high hill. It stood regally in the midst of rolling velvet lawns and flower beds that were just beginning to come awake in the early spring sunshine.

Mr. Radcliff called the new arrival Randy, the same name he had given to all his other dogs. After the puppy was housebroken by the butler, he was allowed the run of the house. It was a spacious place with many carpeted rooms and an abundance of armchairs and couches—the dream of any energetic, mischievous puppy.

It was an adult home Randy had come to, and a

rather cold one. Mrs. Radcliff openly disliked dogs, and Mr. Radcliff's interest in them was one of possession rather than love. Randy sensed this and avoided them both, but he got along well with everyone else. Annie, the cook, usually had a delectable tidbit for him, and the chauffeur always had a kind word. But the puppy had little real companionship. The only member of the household who played with him occasionally was Mr. Brenner, the old gardener, who also scolded whenever he found him digging in the flower beds.

By October, Randy had become a truly beautiful golden retriever. He had settled down quite a bit. Now that he was a year old, he wore a leather collar with his name engraved on the brass plate affixed to it.

Randy was a loner who sat on the front lawn a good part of the day watching an occasional car or a horseback rider go by. He sometimes trotted down the long graveled driveway to the dirt road to stand at its edge, gazing off into the distance. But he never roamed away from the house.

He was a quiet, good-natured dog, seemingly happy and contented. His first winter with the Radcliffs was spent mostly indoors or down below the house where he could survey the frozen pond and the neighborhood children skating on the far side.

But in early April, when the green began filtering up through the brown fields, the golden-coated dog became restless, and soon he was spending more time in the surrounding countryside than on his front lawn. Often when he did not show up for dinner, his owner dispatched the chauffeur to look for him. The man usually found him wandering aimlessly along one of the many roads that crisscrossed the area. When the chauffeur called, Randy obediently got into the limousine and rode home sitting quietly in the back seat.

As spring became summer, Randy drifted further away from the Radcliff house. Sometimes when he returned after being absent for a day or two his owner locked him in the kennel for a while, hoping this might dampen his wanderlust. But the moment the dog was released, he was off again.

The countryside was spotted with farms and groups of small houses. Randy got to know the residents and before long most of them became familiar with the handsome golden retriever whose warm, friendly manner charmed all who met him.

"Hi, Randy!" the children would cry as he came trotting up to them. He accepted their welcome with a great show of tail wagging, grinning broadly as small hands reached out to him. He was never pushy or overbearing, and when he had had enough, he moved on up the road.

When he met strange dogs, he stood his ground in a manner that was neither aggressive nor defensive and none ever tried to stand in his way.

The golden dog stopped in occasionally to visit the Radcliffs, who had just about given up on him. Mr.

Radcliff, however, was still hopeful that one day Randy would get over his roving ways and come back to stay.

But Randy was his own dog now. He made no attachments. He had become a drifter, an amiable tramp. Yet, anyone watching the purposeful way he trotted across the fields or up the middle of a road might feel that here was a dog in search of something.

The Lucas farm lay in a small valley about two miles away from the Radcliff residence. It was owned and operated by young Warren Lucas, who took great pride in his fine milch cows and immaculately kept cowbarn and outbuildings.

One morning in the middle of July, Randy stopped at the gate where the two Lucas children were playing quietly in the driveway in front of the low white farmhouse. Behind them a number of geese and white ducks quacked in the barnyard. On the far hillside beyond, a scattering of sheep grazed peacefully. In the adjoining meadows, black-and-white spotted cows rested in dark groups in the shade of the willow trees.

Perhaps the complete tranquillity of the scene held the dog there. For a moment he seemed unable to make up his mind whether to go on or join the children. Then suddenly, waving his golden plume aloft, he bounded up to the little boy and girl. He seemed to be grinning from ear to ear, as if to say, "Here I am. Aren't you lucky I've come to visit you!"

The visit became a stay. The children fell in love

with their new pet immediately, and it certainly looked as if Randy had no intention of leaving. Warren Lucas checked with some of his neighbors about the dog's identity. They all remembered seeing him around but the brass plate on his collar only said that his name was Randy, nothing else.

The Radcliff chauffeur spotted the golden retriever on the Lucas front lawn a short time later. He recognized the dog instantly and brought him home. Two days later Randy was back with the Lucases. The chauffeur picked him up again, and Randy returned to the Lucas family again.

This back-and-forth game went on through the month of August. At times, Randy returned to the Lucas farm every day. More often, two or three days elapsed before he made it back.

One evening in the beginning of September, Mr. Radcliff phoned Warren Lucas.

"Look here, sir," he announced. His voice was more annoyed than angry. "My chauffeur has picked up my dog at your place over twenty times this past month. That's getting a bit ridiculous, don't you think?"

"I'm sorry about that," the farmer replied, "but what can I do about it?"

"Not much, I suppose," Mr. Radcliff answered, "but I think that the best thing for me to do at this point is give him to you!"

Warren Lucas and his comely, red-haired wife, Betty, were delighted to accept this beautiful gift, and of course the children were overjoyed. Randy was now officially theirs, and for a while it seemed that the golden retriever had found what he was looking for at last.

The Lucas dairy farm had everything that Randy loved—cows, pigs, sheep, chickens, geese, and flocks of doves that zoomed constantly over the barnyard or lined up like white banners along the crest of the barn roof. In the mornings the dog joined his new owner in the cowshed while the milking machines were in action.

The young farmer became extremely fond of Randy, as he could not help but respond to the retriever's friendliness. And although the dog still romped with the children after school, he seemed to have become their father's companion. He followed the farmer about as he did his chores and frequently rode beside him in the cab of the pickup truck. But Warren Lucas knew dogs and he recognized in this one a certain independence and a touch of aloofness that somehow kept them apart.

The snow came early in December, banking against the farm buildings and blocking the driveways. Randy began to trail along behind the tractor as Warren Lucas pushed the drifts aside. In the winter evenings, Betty Lucas would prepare Randy's dinner, and afterward the dog would stretch out before the fireplace, perhaps dreaming of the places he'd been or of adventures yet to come.

The "January thaw" came in the second week of February. The mud was knee deep for three days; then winter seemed to start all over again. March blew in with a tremendous snowstorm and the drifts did not begin to melt until the end of the month.

Then, one morning in early April, Randy walked out the driveway and turned east.

Warren Lucas saw him leave. He called out, "Hey, Randy, come back!" But Randy was on his way.

That evening the children asked where the dog had gone.

Their father stood by the window gazing in the direction Randy had taken. All that afternoon he had been watching, hoping against hope. He smiled sadly at the youngsters.

"Randy has got spring fever," he said as he filled his pipe. "He has the urge to travel on—maybe he'll come back."

But in his heart he knew that Randy never would.

All through the following summer Randy shifted from one place to the next, covering an area of approximately twenty square miles. He rarely went hungry, as most people were pleased to give him food when he came to the door. How could they resist the charming individual with the golden coat? Some tried to entice him to stay on, but to no avail.

Actually, Randy was a strange dog—outgoing, affable, but still basically a loner. He did not join any of the dogs that roamed about and never ran deer or other wild game. He was constantly on the move—seemingly lighthearted yet somehow haunted by some obscure force that pushed him ever onward, allowing him no time to settle down or take root anywhere.

On an afternoon in September, Randy was proceeding north along the shoulder of a hardtop road just south of the county line.

The day was extremely hot and humid for September. Randy was thirsty and, to add to his discomfort, police cars began appearing, driving slowly past him, going in both directions. Automobiles never bothered Randy. Right from the beginning of his travels he had learned to keep out of their way. But these cars had speakers that blared loudly and abrasively. Finally, ears tucked back, he turned off the road into the woods. He met an old cowpath and followed it downhill to a narrow strip of marshland. Here he lay in a shallow stream for a little while, lapping the water and feeling the wet coolness against his belly. Later he got up, shook himself, and wandered across a brush-covered field to an abandoned apple orchard on the far side. Now he could no longer hear the loudspeakers. Up ahead beyond the orchard the woods became almost impenetrable with windfalls and tangles of vines. Randy skirted them, then swung upgrade to pick up the road once more where the going would be easier.

A whimpering sound stopped him in his tracks. With lowered head, he stalked cautiously forward to

investigate and suddenly came face to face with a small boy. The child was standing alone in a mass of green ferns. His blond hair was plastered against his forehead and tear-stained cheeks. His blue shirt, ripped by thorns, hung limply against his small body.

The four-year-old had been lost in the woods since early that morning when he had wandered away from his home to pick berries.

The police loudspeakers had been calling him: "Billy, come to the road! Billy, come to the road!" But Billy could not hear them, and even if he had, he would not have known where the road was.

To Randy, the youngster was no different from the many other children he had met. And Randy's wagging tail and grinning face told Billy this was a friend.

A friend was what Billy needed now more than anything in the world. His little hands reached out to clutch the leather collar, and Randy started off in the direction he had been going. Because he was a "gentleman" and in no hurry, he walked slowly to allow the boy to keep up. At one time the child stumbled and let go. Randy stopped and waited for him to rise and take hold once more.

After almost an hour, the pair emerged from the woods onto the road. Minutes later a patrol car pulled up alongside them. A policeman got out and picked up the child. He held the back door open for Randy, who leaped in without a moment's hesitation. He had ridden in a limousine at one time, and a pickup truck not too long ago. As far as he was concerned, a patrol car was no different.

They arrived in front of a small farmhouse a short time later. There were other automobiles parked in the driveway near several people. Billy's mother came rushing to the police car when she saw her son in the front seat beside the officer. She wept with joy when she held the child in her arms.

"Oh, you found him! You found him!" she cried over and over again.

The officer smiled.

"It wasn't me that found your boy, ma'am," he declared. "It was this dog that did it!"

He pointed to Randy. "Saw them both come out of the woods together, the dog leading and the boy hanging on."

Of course Randy became an instant hero. He did not know what great feat he had accomplished, but he was not one to question the praise and adoration he was suddenly receiving.

He was invited into Billy Armor's home and given an enormous meal, the like of which he had not had in a long time. That evening a reporter came to the house with notebook and camera, and the following weekend a picture of Billy and Randy appeared in the local newspaper with the story of how this wonderful dog had rescued the lost child.

Randy lived with the Armors for more than two weeks. Mrs. Armor wanted to keep him but felt it her duty to find out who owned this treasure. She made constant inquiries and ran an ad in the lost-and-found section of the newspaper, but there were no answers.

She groomed the dog every day until his coat took on an added golden luster. The family would have been delighted if Randy had chosen to live with them forever but, one cool afternoon in the beginning of October, Randy hit the trail once more.

All that morning he had been sitting in front of the Armors' house with his nose lifted to the wind. Huge swirls of blowing leaves whipped across the grass and heaped against the front porch in fluttering mounds of yellow and red. Just after noon, Randy meandered out the open gate of the front yard and turned south along the same road he had been following north just a few weeks earlier.

High overhead a formation of Canada geese

53

preceded him. The sky was overcast, with the sun breaking through occasionally to splash its brightness across the land.

Randy quickened his pace as the faint honking notes of the migrating birds reached him, urging him on.

Katie Conklin lived in a dilapidated brown house along one of the many dirt roads that wound its way through the center of the county. She was a small woman, thin and slightly bent. There was an allover gray look about her—shoes, faded print dress, hair. But her eyes, deep set and dark, belied the drabness of her appearance.

She had been born in this house. It had been a working farm then. The barn had been occupied by a team of Clydesdales and many cows, and the summer fields had been green with corn. She had especially loved the time of haying and late August when vegetables and fruits were put up for the winter. But after her husband was killed in a tractor accident, the farm deteriorated rapidly, for they had no children to carry on. Katie continued to live there with an older sister. The two women could sometimes be seen walking slowly together down to an isolated country store where they did their shopping.

After her sister died, Katie was rarely seen outdoors again. She survived on a small income that had been left to her in a family will, and the only one who ever looked in on the old woman was an elderly black man who came up from the store to bring her food.

Katie had become a recluse. She was completely alone. Day after day she sat by her kitchen window and stared out at the changing seasons. Now it was early autumn. The days were still warm, but lately in the morning there was frost in the long valley below the house.

For the past week Katie had been aware that a beautiful, golden-colored dog was in the area. Once she had seen it go by on the road, and just the day before she had noticed him, moving along the fence line behind the barn

He made her think of a small brown dog she had had when she was a child—it seemed so long ago. Way back in the recesses of her memory she could almost see him—leaping, barking with joy whenever they met.

All the following morning Katie sat on her porch hoping to see the golden dog again. He did not appear that day or the next, but on the afternoon of the third day she saw him from her bedroom window—this time trotting up the road, heading in the direction of her house.

Katie quickly wrapped a shawl around her shoulders and hurried down the porch steps to the edge of the road.

As Randy came along, she stooped forward and reached out her hand.

"Hey, big dog," she called softly.

Randy turned toward her and stopped just beyond her reach. In the past he had only been approached like this by children. He seemed suspicious for a moment, but because he had such a good-natured, friendly character he walked up to the gray-haired woman and allowed her fingers to stroke the top of his head gently.

Katie's hand touched his collar. She turned her head to one side and squinted her eyes so that she could read the brass plate more easily. She rubbed its surface with her thumb to clear off the grime it had accumulated.

"My, you have a beautiful name," she breathed. "A long time ago," she revealed, smiling, "I had a dog like you—not as pretty perhaps, but he was a nice dog and I loved him very much."

Tears welled into her eyes. "I remember now," she went on. "I called him Willy—strange that I should forget such a simple name."

Randy did not understand a word she was saying but something held him there. He closed his eyes, panting softly, as Katie's gentle hand caressed the thick fur of his shiny coat.

"How would you like to come in for a drink of water?" she asked. "You look warm."

The old woman straightened up and turned back to her house.

Randy remained standing where he was. He seemed puzzled—and uncertain. Then he followed her up the porch steps and sat back on his haunches facing the door.

Katie went inside and quickly returned with a bowl

of cool water. She placed it on the floor in front of him. The dog was not thirsty but he took a few courteous laps.

Afterward he returned to the road and continued on his way. He looked back once to see Katie still on the porch, her pale face turned toward him, her hand raised to shield her eyes from the sun just going down behind the trees.

Randy returned two days later. Since he had left Katie Conklin, he had been wandering through the countryside. But instead of moving on, an unexplainable compulsion seemed to draw him back to the old woman.

He approached Katie's house from the field behind it late in the day. The sun had already set, but a pink afterglow remained. It was the hour of silhouettes when the distant hills become deep purple and the trees are etched in black against the sky.

A faint yellow light appeared in one of the windows as Randy came up to the back porch and lay down. The evening was warm and soon the air was alive with the sounds of the forest.

The door suddenly opened and Katie came out. She seated herself in a rocking chair, then discerned Randy in the gloom below her.

She was not startled. It was almost as if she expected him to be there.

"Good evening, Randy," she said quietly. "Why don't you come up and sit here beside me?"

She held out her hand and Randy came up to it, ducking his head slightly so that her fingers could reach the soft fur of his neck. They sat there together until the evening deepened into night and the stars glittered overhead.

The old woman had given up. She had turned inward. She had separated herself from the outside world and had allowed her utter loneliness and despair to take over. Now for the first time in years she was conscious of a new warmth within her and a wondrous feeling of peace and contentment.

Katie opened her eyes. She had fallen asleep, but the chill night air awakened her. The golden dog was no longer there. She peered into the darkness and called his name, then finally rose to her feet and walked slowly back into the house.

The following night Randy came by again. It had

turned cold and this time Katie invited him to come in. But Randy preferred to stay on the porch. Katie spread out an old blanket for him to lie on, and in the morning she rose early to feed him a bowl of warm porridge which she had prepared the night before.

These visits went on into the middle of November. They became more and more frequent. Each time Randy went away, Katie eagerly looked forward to his return. She also bought a large bag of dog food so that he could have a good meal when he arrived.

They began taking short walks together. The old woman moved slowly, and when Randy got too far ahead, he waited for her to catch up.

Before long he came into the house and slept beside her bed every night, stretched out on a large flowered pad she had made for him. She also bought herself a warm mackinaw and new, comfortable shoes.

Soon they were walking together every day. The old woman stepped more briskly now to keep up with her dog. Randy shortened his stride to help her.

When spring came, with the aid of a neighbor, Katie put in a vegetable garden and planted flowers along the front of the house. Later that summer she had the house painted white with green trim.

Randy never roamed again. Everyone had thought he was just a lovable tramp who followed an endless trail to nowhere. But the truth of the matter appears to be that Randy had indeed been in search of something—someone who really needed him. When he found Katie Conklin, he was content to spend the rest of his life with her.

Paragon

I JUST ABOUT flipped when Mrs. Trenley asked me to ride her horse Paragon at Piping Ridge, the first of the big outdoor shows of the season.

In her youth Mrs. Trenley had been a top rider, but now her hair was snow white and, even though she still went fox-hunting, she did not show much any more. However, her stable boasted some of the best horses on the eastern circuit. To be asked to show one was the dream of every rider—especially if he was only eighteen and just getting started in the business. This could be my big break, the beginning of a career I had been aiming at for the past three years.

It had been quite a while since I last saw Paragon. He had been off on the Florida circuit, but before that I had visited him almost every day. Mrs. Trenley's stable was just over the hill from where we lived. I remembered Paragon when he was romping in the pasture with the other foals. He had caught my eye right from the beginning—that bright chestnut color and the white stripe running down the middle of his face. I had watched him grow into a beautiful yearling. Joe Yance, Mrs. Trenley's trainer, broke the colt and schooled him just before he turned three.

Yance once said to me, "This colt is going to make a terrific show hunter. He's bold, big striding, and will jump any fence you point him at."

I was only a pony clubber at the time but in my heart I yearned for the day I could ride and show this beautiful horse. And now that day had come sooner than I expected. Bill Richardson, Mrs. Trenley's regular rider, had come down with the flu. That was the reason she phoned to ask if I could fill in for him. She said she had watched me in some of the local shows and felt that I could give her horse a good ride. And that I was determined to do—give her horse a good ride.

I arrived at the showgrounds early and met the Trenley horse van when it pulled into the parking area. As I watched the red gelding come down the ramp, the anticipation of the day ahead made me tingle all over.

"Hi, Paragon. Remember me?"

I reached out and stroked the silky neck. He swung his head around and cuffed me gently on the shoulder.

"By gosh, he does remember you," chuckled Clancy, the groom, as he undid the horse's leg wraps and tail cover.

Paragon raised his head, the small curvy ears twitching nervously as he surveyed the bustling excitement of the show grounds. The long arched neck, the good sloping shoulder, the short back and solid quarters and clean hard legs—everything about him was thoroughbred. He had grown since I had last seen him. When I caught the stirrup iron and lifted myself to his back, I figured his height at sixteen two and as I gently settled into the saddle, the feel of him against my legs was just right.

I picked up my number at the information booth and slipped it on my arm. I warmed up Paragon in the outdoor ring, circling it three or four times at a walk, then at a trot. His stride was long, but quick and even, with a nice rhythmic bounce that made it easy to post. We stopped, backed, cantered on both leads, then left the ring and jogged across the fast-filling grounds to the outside course where riders were schooling their mounts over the jumps before the show began. So far so good. My horse was soft in my hand with a smooth, easy response to my leg that promised a good day.

It was then that Jack Donahue rode up alongside me. He was a lean, red-haired guy who sat his horse with an arrogance that had always made me feel inadequate.

"Who are you riding, Scotty boy?" Jack asked in that smug way of his, as though I were just a wet-nosed kid and he Jack Donahue the Great.

"Paragon, one of Mrs. Trenley's horses," I answered quietly, careful to keep the exuberance out of my voice. I was completely unprepared for the bucket of ice Donahue promptly dumped on my head.

"Did you say *Paragon?* For Pete's sake, Scotty, that horse will kill you!"

"What do you mean, kill me?" I tried to sound disinterested but there was a slight tremor in my voice.

Donahue must have noticed it for he smiled and lit up a cigarette. "Wait till you jump him!" He laughed as he cantered on ahead.

Jack did not bother to acquaint his horse with the obstacles as the other riders did but went on into his first fence at a gallop. He crossed it smoothly and efficiently like the expert he was, then jumped the rest —all eight with the same split-haired timing that had made him one of the top ten riders on the eastern circuit. He let his horse move on after the last fence. The cigarette was still dangling from his smiling lips as he pulled up and came to a halt right in front of me. His eyes said, "Beautiful, wasn't it?" I was about to agree but before I could open my mouth, Donahue cut me down again.

"As I was saying," Jack continued, "wait till you school that horse. You'll find out what I mean. He charges his fences, then chickens out and climbs over instead of jumping. He put Bill Richardson in the hospital down in Miami; then two weeks later at Ridgeland he turned over on a coop and clobbered Bill again real good. No, sir, I wouldn't ride that red hunk of nothing for a million bucks. Now, you don't think Bill really has the flu," he added confidentially. "He's scared of the horse, he . . ."

I left Jack talking to himself and walked Paragon up to the first fence—an aiken, brush with rail on top. My heart was thumping madly and I felt as if I had a wad of cotton in my mouth. I let my horse stand and look at the jump for a second, then wheeled away and came around in a wide circle. Paragon broke into a gallop about thirty feet before the obstacle. I asked him to take off too soon, causing him to grab an extra stride and get in too close. The jump was high, straight up and straight down, and when we landed I was straddling his ears.

I quickly shinnied back down to where I belonged. I collected my horse and crumbling confidence and walked up to the next fence. We went through the same routine, only this time I managed to stay in the saddle. I couldn't figure out what was going wrong. The next four fences were just as bad. Paragon came in either too close or stood off too far. We just weren't getting together. Our timing was off. I walked him in between fences because he was beginning to fret and pull and I was afraid if I let him move out he would get away from me.

The last fence was an in-and-out—two parallel posts and rail fences twenty-eight feet apart. The only way to negotiate this obstacle was jump in, one stride, and jump out. It was easy if you did it that way. But it took a mighty clever horse to get in wrong and come out right. As we approached, I hoped that Paragon was that kind because three strides back I knew he was coming in wrong. He did, too, and quit—then changed his mind and jumped. He barely cleared the in. He came to ground on all four feet at once, then took off from a standstill and lunged for the out. But

his pace was gone. The rails blew up as he crashed through them and I hit the ground so hard my coat buttons popped.

It took three men over five minutes to get that fence put together and almost that long for me to get my wind back. Paragon wasn't hurt, just shook up. I went over him very carefully to make sure. I couldn't believe what was happening. Only a short time ago I had been bursting with confidence—right now it seemed that all of it was rapidly draining out my boots.

Like the voice of doom, the loudspeaker boomed,

"Clear the outside course. First class coming up—open working hunter."

Each rider peeled off and took the course as his number was called. But I was hardly aware of them. I sat there in a blue funk with my heart that close to my mouth that, if I spit, I'd lose it. There were no two ways about it—I was afraid—afraid of this horse and what he might do to me. This was only the first class with three more to go. How could I possibly survive them with this four-legged counterfeit under me? "Paragon, how can you do this to me? You were my dream horse—I was counting on you but you've let me down."

When my number was called, I came through the ingate, circled once, and let Paragon move out into the first fence. He took it and the next four badly, getting in too close and leaping over each as if it were ten feet high. The fifth fence was a wooden coop. Paragon came in off stride. He jumped too soon, then reached desperately for a safe landing. But his back legs struck timber with tremendous impact, sending his hindquarters skyward and his nose downward. I was sure the end had come but the red horse recovered somehow and scrambled for fifty feet, trying to keep his balance. I didn't help him one bit for I was draped over his neck like a lead necklace. My body began sliding to one side. Somebody was yelling, "Stay on! Stay on!" but I was too far gone. I struck the earth on my seat. My hard hat spun off my head as I cartwheeled backward and slid to a halt, face buried in the turf with my arms and legs spread to either side as if I'd been staked there. I turned over on my back and stared up at the gray sky. Somebody leaned over me and said, "Stay where you are!"

I clenched my fingers and wriggled my toes and came to the conclusion that everything was still work-ing. Carefully I rolled to my knees and got to my feet, then stood there shakily for a moment trying to brush off the green stains and brown earth that were ground into my clothes. Someone had caught Paragon and he handed me the reins and my helmet. My horse's nose was also streaked with dirt. We walked slowly from the field to the vans parked across the road.

I prayed I would not meet Mrs. Trenley but she was waiting for me.

"Are you all right, Scotty?" Her voice was grave with concern.

"I'm okay," I replied dubiously, for I wasn't sure. Then suddenly in a flash I knew how to get out of all this.

"But I think there's something wrong with Para-gon." I placed my hand on his back directly behind the cantle of the saddle. As I pressed, the red horse winced so badly he almost sat down.

"Oh, dear, his kidneys. I had better get the vet at once."

She left me there with Paragon and hurried toward the judges' booth. The chestnut stood with his head cocked to one side, eyeing me—and he had good rea-son. Horses will wince slightly under pressure on the kidneys, and what Mrs. Trenley had not noticed, but the red horse had, was the way I pressed down—with all my might.

Old Doc Kearney came up with Mrs. Trenley. He was a taciturn man but a good vet, and one look into the pale blue eyes behind the horn-rimmed glasses told me at once I'd have to get up pretty early in the morning to outsmart this guy.

I stripped the saddle off and the doctor went over Paragon carefully, poking here, pressing there. When he finally turned to Mrs. Trenley, I felt he was addressing me.

"There is nothing wrong with this horse," he said slowly, "not a goldarn thing!"

Our next class was hunter hack—walk, trot, and canter, no jumping. The horse to be judged mainly on manners and way of going. I was sure we'd pick up a ribbon here but Paragon exploded twice right under the judge's nose. And that finished that.

My second trip around the outside course was disaster on horseback. Paragon shut off at the third fence and I could not get him over. The third refusal automatically eliminated us but the judge suggested I jump it before leaving the course. We battled out there for ten minutes—until the turf looked as if a tractor had been spinning on it. I was humiliated and demoralized. The red horse reared and bucked and suddenly lit out across the field as though he'd been blown out of a cannon. I hauled back on the reins for all I was worth but he had his head down and try as I might I couldn't raise it. We jumped the outgate and crossed the road running flat out. People scattered before us, some yelling advice but most climbing cars and fences to give us clearance. Paragon was heading for the van like a homing pigeon. He took the ramp in one bound, slid across the floor on his haunches, then turned sideways and slammed against the padded wall with a mighty crash. Clancy helped extricate me from where I clung to the chestnut's topside, sandwiched between the horse and the van roof. When I staggered out through the open door my helmet was gone and my coat hung from my shoulders in two parts, ripped right down the back. Fortunately or unfortunately for me, Mrs. Trenley wasn't around. If she had witnessed this performance, I would have been grounded right then and there.

The noon break was announced. The sun came out but I was too miserable to appreciate it. I couldn't eat a thing. Clancy made me down some coffee but I threw it up five minutes after I drank it.

Clancy went off and I slumped down on the ramp. Paragon stood tied to the van as we both waited for the first afternoon class. I was trapped. There was no way out.

This whole situation baffled me. It was unreasonable. Paragon had been campaigned for two years. He had won several championships and many blues, and yet our performance this morning had been pure calamity.

I'd always been taught, "It is never the horse's

fault!" If this was true, then the fault had to be mine.

I got to my feet and walked up to Paragon. He backed to the end of his tie line. When I rested my hand on his shoulder, I could feel the tension in him. I reached up and scratched the cowlick on his forehead until he relaxed and closed his eyes with the sheer pleasure of it.

"If you could only talk my friend. If you could only tell me . . ."

The loudspeaker blared forth.

"First afternoon class. Working hunter. Gentleman to ride!"

Clancy had pinned my coat together and he helped me into it. I mounted like an old man and rode slowly toward the outside course. This time the red horse quit ten feet before the first fence. I was thankful Mrs. Trenley was not present to see it. There was no heart left in me—no fight at all. I was yellow, gutless, washed up—just about as low-down as a guy can get. As I led Paragon off the field not a sound came from the spectators.

For the "lady-to-ride" Paragon was scratched. He had to be. After his three performances that day, there wasn't a lady this side of heaven who'd come near him with a ten-foot pole.

The thousand dollar stake was the last class of the day—the most spectacular. It called for brilliance. Only those horses that could gallop on and jump big had any hope of success. Paragon didn't have a chance with me in the saddle, and Mrs. Trenley knew it.

"Scotty." She spoke softly. We were standing in the shadow of the van with the late afternoon sun going down behind it. "I think you've had enough." There was sadness in her voice, and regret that I had muffed things so badly. I stood in front of her with my face hanging down to my boots, my eyes on the ground, unable to meet hers. Of course she was right and there wasn't a darn thing left for me to say.

"Perhaps I can get Jack Donahue to ride Paragon in the stake," she went on. "Last night he was eager to."

My heart began pounding against my ribs as if I'd been running.

"Mrs. Trenley," I cut in, "would you repeat that? Did you say that *last night* Donahue asked if he could show Paragon?"

"Why, yes, but I told him I'd already asked you."

So that was it! That lying double-crosser had tricked me, jinxed me. He wouldn't ride the red horse for a million bucks—so he *said.* He had baited me and I swallowed the whole works. It all came clear now. Donahue had planned this. He knew I was green, unsure of myself, and he made the most of it. Realization of the truth and a wave of guilt hit me squarely between the eyes. It wasn't Paragon who had goofed at all. It wasn't Paragon who let me down. It was I who let him down. More than anything else in the world he had needed my confidence to send him on and let him do his job. But I had stymied and frustrated him every inch of the way. I blew up and clashed controls. I asked him to move on, then hung back—saying go and stop in the same breath. Now the poor horse was completely confused, but only because *I* had confused him. I was disgusted with myself for being such a dupe and I was mad, too—sizzling mad.

I overtook Mrs. Trenley halfway to the announcer's booth. I blocked her path and grabbed both her arms as though I'd gone off my rocker.

"Mrs. Trenley," I pleaded, "let me ride Paragon in the stake—please! I know I goofed all day but I'm okay now. Give me one more chance—please give me one more chance."

She looked down at my hands and I dropped them quickly to my sides. She studied me a long moment, perhaps measuring this ball of fire against the stumblebum who'd been lousing up her horse all day. She came to a decision.

"All right, Scotty," she said. "Go ahead, you may as well finish it."

"Thank you," I cried and was off and running toward the van before the words were out of my mouth.

Paragon was tacked up and waiting as I came charging up. Clancy was at his head—hand on the bridle, holding him steady. I swung into the saddle with new bounce. Across the showgrounds the "stake horses" were assembling at the outside course. I sent Clancy to the announcer's booth to have my number shoved to the bottom of the list. We needed time, for between now and when we negotiated the course again, the damage I had inflicted on Paragon had to be undone.

There was no room left for nerves. Within the next

twenty minutes a new working relationship had to be established between me and the red horse. To accomplish this, I chose an open area within earshot of the loudspeakers. I stopped Paragon and asked him to back, then legged him forward and backed again. We repeated this exercise several times. I was softening my horse—teaching him to come back to the subtle pull on the rein and to go forward instantly when he felt the soft pressure of my legs.

I had once heard William Steinkraus of the United States Equestrian Team say, "Never lie to your horse. He must believe in you and must understand that he will not hurt himself if he does what you ask of him."

I was aware that I had been lying to my horse all day. Because of my own lack of courage, I had robbed the horse of his. I had caused Paragon to fall and rear and buck, and finally run off in a last effort to escape the idiot on his back. Now in minutes with time rapidly running out, I was trying to restore my horse's faith in me.

We cantered the field once, then did it again at a gallop, establishing the pace we would sustain over the outside course. I legged my horse up to a stone wall, then backed him thirty feet and sent him forward into it. Because Paragon was still not sure of me, he came in too close but popped over it. No stake class was ever won with that kind of jumping. Speed and good clean fencing was the only combination that could possibly keep us in the ribbons.

I tried the stone wall again. This time I tapped the

horse with the crop when I felt we were right for take off. Paragon responded and sailed over cleanly with plenty of air on both sides of the wall. Good enough. We were getting there. My signals were now definite and clean cut with nothing left to chance.

We were in the center of the field once more. I could hear the loudspeaker blaring away but my number had not yet been called. One more thing to do. I held my horse in place, then clucked with my tongue and used the bat simultaneously. Paragon responded to the stick by moving forward the instant it touched his flank. I repeated this performance, only this time I did not use the stick. Now the circuit was complete because Paragon responded to my voice without employing the crop. From here on out I would not only have hands and legs for control but also my voice.

We had finished our schooling just in time. The loudspeaker called, "Number 72—Paragon, ridden by Scott O'Leary, next over the outside course."

"That's for us, red horse!"

I swung him toward the ingate. He knew I was on his side now. His neck was arched into the bit—feeling it but not pulling, and his quarters came well under in smooth powerful thrusts that told me he was as ready now as he ever would be.

We approached the course slowly. The steward signaled all clear and as we cantered by I let Paragon stretch into a smooth ground-eating gallop. The first fence came at us like an express train. Now we could do no wrong for my quaking guts were gone—forgotten—and all that mattered was this moment and this job to be done. At last we were a team, synchronized, working together, flying the fences, taking them in stride as we met them—millbrook, white gate, stone wall. I felt his hocks drive in under as I brought him back going into the turn. Steady, red horse, steady. . . . Easy does it . . . angle left into the wooden coop, hold your line. That's it . . . now! And the coop was past. The terrain dipped and swung upward. Paragon, his neck straight out, was really moving. My eyes were fixed on the horizon but in the perimeter of my vision, below me, I could see his knees like red pistons driving the earth past in a green blur, then reaching for more . . . more . . . then over the snake fence and up the long slope to the in-and-out etched against the blue sky like a fortress.

We came zooming in at breathtaking speed. Thirty feet away I knew we were wrong. My legs drove against him, and as he lengthened his stride I clucked and turned his head loose. This was our moment of truth. If he ran out or shut off now I'd have jumped the in without him. But his confidence had returned. I had said, "Go on, you can do it," and Paragon did. He came up under me, lifting us over together, then one stride, and jump again with room to spare. And that was it!

A rousing cheer exploded around us as we came barreling through. I came up in my irons and let Paragon roll on, then slow down gradually. I spotted

Donahue sulking in the saddle and glaring at me with such vehemence that if looks could kill I'd have dropped dead right there.

I pulled up my horse in the shade of a giant oak. He was still charged up, prancing like a colt, swishing his tail, flinging white foam from his tossing head.

As if a gray veil had been lifted, suddenly the grass was greener with the air so sweet, so sharp I could hardly breathe. Sweat stung my eyes and lips, coursing downward to my shoulders, soaking my shirt, washing me—drowning all the misery and frustration of the long day. I slid to the ground and loosened the girth. My knees were spongy under me. I threw an arm over Paragon's neck for support. His head swung around and cuffed me on the shoulder and I knew we were friends once more.

Mrs. Trenley hugged me so hard the pins holding my coat together popped open and my good luck tie-pin pinched the skin on my chest.

Later, after the trophy and the prize money were awarded, Mrs. Trenley said, "Scotty, that was one of the finest stake rounds I have ever seen. I'm very proud of you. You got off to a bad start this morning, but you came through in great style."

She paused for a moment, then added, "You know, Paragon is not an easy horse to ride. He is a talented, temperamental individual, but you finally found the key to him."

I nodded and smiled with no comment, for only I knew that what I had really found was the key to myself.

Kelly

As SECOND LIEUTENANT David Martin came striding up to the Fort Ord bachelor officers' quarters, the enlisted man standing in the doorway snapped to attention and saluted.

The young officer returned the salute and smiled down at the large black and tan shepherd pup that lay at the soldier's feet.

"Good-looking dog you've got there," he commented, then asked, "Were you waiting to see me?"

"Yes, sir, I was," the soldier answered. "I'm Private Frank Kelly, 92nd Infantry."

The pup sat up, and the fingers of Private Kelly's left hand began fondling the straight black ears.

"Sergeant Jackson of your company told me you might like a dog," the G.I. continued. "You see, sir, our outfit has been alerted. We're moving out any day now, and I've got to find a home for this one."

Dave knew what Kelly was about to say, but waited for him to finish.

"He's a good dog, housebroken and everything, and only ten months old. Corporal Day gave him to me a couple of months ago when his outfit pulled out."

The first words that sprang to Dave's lips were, "No, thanks, what in the world would I do with a dog out here in California?" But there was something about this pup that reminded him of his grandmother's Rex back East in Pennsylvania. In one fleeting instant his mind bridged the gap of years. Rex had been a collie, the old-fashioned kind with prick ears, broad forehead and deep-set eyes, but this dog had the same eager look and awakened in Dave familiar, unfulfilled yearnings of another time.

Private Kelly, obviously sensing that Dave was faltering, quickly reached for the opening.

"Honest, Lieutenant, you'll love him. Everyone just calls him 'the pup' so you can name him anything you like. He's still a little scary, ain't been around too much, but he'll get over that. All he needs is someone to take him along and he'll become one terrific dog, I promise you." His blue eyes began to lose their anxious expression as Dave bent to pet the dog.

Later, Dave was glad that he had named the black pup Kelly, because Private Frank Kelly died in action on Attu and the shepherd became a monument to his memory.

Dave bought his dog a collar with a brass plate on which was inscribed: "PFC Kelly, Company B, 352nd

Engineers." The engraver left room around the single chevron for future promotion.

Captain Rhome, the company commander, informed his lieutenant that if Kelly were to move in with them, he had to be properly disciplined.

So Dave and his dog enrolled in a dog obedience class that was held every Monday night in the high-school gymnasium in Monterey, just a few miles from the post.

The beginner's class was a riot of sound and confusion. There were some dogs, including Kelly, who forgot they were housebroken, but in a very short time they all settled down and went to work. "Heel. . . . Sit. . . . Stay. . . . Come. . . . Down . . . ," over and over again, until Dave was rattling the commands off in his sleep and Kelly was probably hearing them in his. They worked together for twenty minutes every evening in the company street with the men looking on—cheering when the dog did well and groaning when he goofed.

Their graduation test included the "long down." Thirty-five dogs were given the command, and dropped to the floor. The lights were turned off and all the owners left the room. Then there were whistles and cat calls, choker chains sliding across the floor, and any number of other distracting noises to tempt the dogs to disobey their masters.

After five minutes, the lights were turned back on. Some dogs were meandering around the gymnasium

and others were sitting up, getting ready to join them. Only nine dogs were still down, just as they had been left—and Kelly was one of the nine.

The following day another chevron was added to the brass collar plate which now read "Corporal Kelly, Company B, 352nd Engineers."

Those school days were great fun and, more significantly, they established a language between Dave and Kelly which was never to be forgotten.

Whenever Dave returned to his quarters after an evening out, Kelly greeted him at the door, then went to his pallet on the floor. Though he was not allowed to sleep on the bed, it was obvious that the big dent in the pillow and the black and tan hairs all over the blanket were not left by a cat.

One evening, Dave let Kelly accompany him on a date. They sat together in the waiting room of the nurses' quarters. When Lieutenant Lorenze came in, Kelly greeted her quietly, then accompanied the pair to the Officers' Club. He lay beside Dave's chair during dinner and sat in the corner of the ballroom, watching the couple as they danced.

Later that evening, the pretty blonde nurse bent down and kissed Kelly smack between the eyes. "What a nice dog you are," she said. "And what a marvelous chaperon!"

"The best chaperon in the world," thought Dave. "He can't talk."

But of course Dave knew that this was not so. Kelly

could talk all right—eyes, ears, tail, every part of him could talk. He had one kind of bark for alarm, another for company coming, still another for play—a whole slew of them, each with its own particular meaning, its own message.

Kelly could also sing. Any man in Company B would have verified that.

Each evening at retreat, four platoons lined up in the company block. Roll call was taken. The bugler stood at the far end of the street with Kelly sitting beside him. As the flag was lowered and the slow mournful notes of retreat echoed in the evening air, Kelly would raise his nose to the heavens and harmonize. Every pitch and variation of the bugle was mimicked by the dog in the saddest duet ever heard.

This unorthodox performance annoyed Captain Rhome. Kelly was locked in the orderly room during the ceremony, but he harmonized from there.

When Stevenson, the bugler, said he did not mind —that before the war he had been accompanied by less capable musicians while playing trumpet with a small band in Los Angeles—Captain Rhome gave in and Kelly became "Apprentice Bugler of Company B."

In six months Kelly had put on weight and filled out. All muscle and bone, he was fit. He was a breeder's version of a German shepherd, from the classic head right down to the tip of the tail, which swung low in a slow curve like a saber, but he was a man's dog. He knew every soldier in the company better than they knew him, and every man in the company was proud of him—even Captain Rhome.

Kelly went along on all field problems, all marches. If the company tramped fifteen miles, Kelly did thirty. He ran on ahead, always scouting, but every now and again he checked in, trotting back down the line of marching men, stopping for a quick nuzzle, a quick pat on the head. There was no doubt that Kelly became as much a part of Company B as any man in it.

Dave prepared to go on leave in March. While he was away, Kelly would continue to sleep in his room but Sergeant Jackson would be in charge of him.

Back home in Pennsylvania, Dave fretted about his dog's welfare. He phoned Sergeant Jackson twice to make sure all was well.

Dave returned to camp one April evening at the end of his furlough. After signing in at the post headquarters, he cut across the parade ground to the bachelor officers' barracks. Suddenly a "wolf" appeared at the edge of the field and came stalking toward him.

"Hi, Kelly," Dave called softly. "Don't you remember me?"

With one joyous yelp, Kelly attacked. The man and the dog rolled over and over on the ground like a pair of wrestling bears. The squeals and groans that erupted from the struggling mass sounded more like a battle than a reunion.

When Dave finally staggered to his feet, laughing

and still trying to fend off his adversary, he saw Sergeant Jackson standing there with a big grin lighting up his boyish face.

"He's your dog, Lieutenant," he declared emphatically. "He belongs to you and you belong to him, and don't let anyone ever tell you different."

Dave was fortunate he had taken his leave when he did. Two days after his return, the battalion was alerted and restricted to the post.

The news was bad—the 92nd Infantry had caught hell in Attu, and things were not going too well in the North African desert. Soldiers in wartime envelope themselves in a protective cloak of immortality. Such grim realities only nick their armor but never penetrate it. The men almost lose sight of why they are in the army and what they are preparing to do. But the orders that came through so quickly shattered the shell of their complacency.

The battalion left Fort Ord to join the regiment in Van Dorn, Mississippi. Kelly went along in the baggage car, but Dave had already begun making plans for his future.

He knew he could not take his dog overseas. There were rules against it. Perhaps his folks in Pennsylvania would keep him, though they really had no room in their small apartment for a dog like Kelly. Dave considered a boarding kennel, but there was no telling when he'd get back—if ever. All sorts of half-baked solutions presented themselves, but Dave discarded them—hedging, stalling. Then something happened that made up his mind.

At the end of April, the battalion went on maneuvers thirty miles north of Colthrop, Mississippi. B Company's objective for the first day was a pillbox, a low, concrete "enemy" fortress on top of a high rise of ground.

The morning was hot, even for Mississippi. In that particular area the weather was always too much of everything, too hot in the summer and too raw cold in the winter. Dave took Kelly along for the ride. He staked him in a relatively cool spot in the bivouac area and, when his platoon pulled out at daybreak, he made sure that his dog had a full bucket of water to keep him company.

He had never tied Kelly before, because he knew that the frustration of it could ruin a dog's disposition. But that morning he did tie him. The operation called for live ammunition and Dave wasn't about to risk Kelly's life on a stray bullet.

About six miles from the bivouac area, the pillbox sat on a grassy knoll, waiting. Dave and Sergeant Jackson crouched in a gully below it. The sun, almost directly overhead, burning downward into the rocky ravine, which was spotted with heavy clumps of scorched brush. The plan of attack was to pin down the pillbox with rifle and machine-gun fire. Two men would rush in with flamethrowers, two more would move in behind them with short-fused satchel charges, place them against the concrete wall of the pillbox, and get away fast before they exploded.

The platoon fanned out and started up the slope, hugging the ground. The stillness of midday was broken only by the distant rumble of gunfire from another battalion operation. Suddenly Dave became aware of a panting behind him. He rolled over on one shoulder as Kelly came loping up, the chewed end of the rope trailing from his collar.

"For Pete's sake," the lieutenant yelled, "you'll get killed out here! Go back, Kelly!"

But Kelly seemed to have forgotten every command Dave had ever taught him. Kelly would not go back; he had come to stay.

It is hard to say how much a dog knows or doesn't know. Maybe Kelly broke training because he was just plain bored—or perhaps his animal sixth sense had foreseen a deadly threat to the man he loved.

The snake had been stretched out flat at the base of a jutting outcrop, but in one split second it was coiled. The flat ugly head was poised at the same level as Dave's, and the harsh penetrating sound of its rattle quivered in the air.

But Kelly ripped in like a thunderbolt as it struck. As in a nightmare, Dave saw the wedge-shaped head meet the dog's right foreleg and heard Kelly's jaws come together with a muffled snap. The earth blew up like a hand grenade and, through the dust, Dave could see the long, lashing body of the snake and the black shep-

herd locked in combat. Kelly's muzzle was clamped
like a steel trap on the writhing reptile. The dog's legs
were braced firmly as his teeth ground into the flesh.

"Enough, Kelly, enough! Let go, Kelly, it's dead.
Leave it. Let go!" Dave was roaring like a madman.

He dove in and grabbed Kelly around the shoulders. The dog let go of the quivering snake as he was
dragged away and flattened out on his side. Dave
quickly slashed an X above the snake bite with his

sheath knife and pressed his mouth down hard on the wound, sucking for all he was worth—sucking, spitting, sucking.

Kelly struggled feebly, then lay still, panting. Dave shouted to Sergeant Jackson to take over the detail and, cradling the dog in his arms, staggered back down the slope. He went to his knees twice and finally reached his jeep, which was parked on a dirt road a quarter of a mile away.

Minutes later, Dave braked to a sliding halt in front of Captain Fannin's tent and, with Kelly in his arms, lurched through the tent doorway before the dust settled.

The regimental doctor was lying on his bunk taking a nap. His thick-lensed glasses, which had slipped down to the tip of his nose, shot across the tent floor as he jerked awake.

"What goes on here?" he muttered as he got up off the bed. He retrieved his spectacles and replaced them, then calmly asked, "What happened to him, Dave?"

"Snake bite—rattler!"

The lieutenant placed Kelly on his side on the table and watched tensely as the doctor gave the dog a huge shot of snake serum. Kelly hardly reacted to the hypodermic needle when it plunged into his rump. The captain listened for a long moment through his stethoscope. Then he attended to the wound and began wrapping a white bandage around the injured leg.

"I think he'll be all right." He grinned at Dave's

worried face. "Be sick for a couple of days, but he'll recover."

"But, Doc," Dave cried, "people *die* from rattlesnake bites!" His stomach was doing flip-flops.

"I know they do—sometimes." The doctor was replacing his instruments in a glass cabinet against the tent wall. "But dogs and most animals don't react the same way to a snake bite as humans do. They seem to have more resistance, and their minds don't dwell on it. No, sir, I wouldn't worry, Dave, he'll be fine."

But Dave did worry, for three days and nights while Kelly lay listlessly in his tent. He managed to coax some water into the dog but could not get him to touch any food.

Dave awoke in the small hours of the fourth morning. As his eyes became accustomed to the gloom, he made out Kelly standing two feet from his cot. He reached out his hand and Kelly came to him, burrowing under his arm, almost lifting him out of the bed. The man and the dog roughhoused gently, quietly, as the tent roof turned gray in the coming dawn.

He was certain now he could not leave his dog. There had to be a way to take him along—as Jackson had said that evening at Fort Ord, they belonged together.

It was Doc Fannin who came up with the solution— a knockout pill before shipping out.

The regiment reached the Charleston Port of Embarkation on a Sunday afternoon. Captain Rhome kept an eagle eye on his company. He was a young man, but everyone referred to him respectfully as the "Old One." He was a rugged individual, tough, spit-and-polish regular army, but human. And even though he suspected that Dave was up to something with Kelly, he did not question his junior officer.

Two days later, stenciled orders came through: "Boarding at midnight." At 11:30 P.M., Kelly swallowed a capsule disguised in a hunk of raw hamburger. Jackson carried Dave's pack and Dave lugged a ninety-pound barracks bag when they climbed the gangplank.

The night was pitch black. A naval officer stood at the rail checking them in. Dave was assigned a stateroom with Lieutenants Condrasky and Lupori. Once inside, he carefully placed the bag on his bunk and opened it. Kelly was snoring like an old man but sleeping like a baby.

Sergeant Jackson came in with Dave's pack. The four men stood in a small, tight semicircle, watching Kelly. Lieutenant Condrasky grinned.

"Now that's what I call neat!" he chuckled.

The ship was a reconverted ocean liner, part of a large convoy strung out and staggered as far as the eye could see. At times Dave felt as though he were cut off from the rest of the world, but periodically he caught a glimpse of their naval escort.

The voyage across the Atlantic was uneventful except for one upsetting incident that occurred when the ship was two weeks out.

Captain MacAlarney, the commanding officer of Company D, disappeared. His roommate, Lieutenant

Griswold, had last seen him at 2200 hours the night before when the captain had stepped out of their stateroom for a breath of fresh air. Griswold turned in without him. When he awoke the next morning, the captain's bunk had not been slept in.

Dave was appointed one of the investigating officers. For the next three days the ship was gone over with a fine-tooth comb. Every soldier and sailor was interrogated, but not one single clue turned up. Captain MacAlarney had simply vanished. No foul play could be proven, but, five days before his disappearance, MacAlarney had found a mascot pup stowed away with his men. While the dog's owner, Corporal Svenson of D Company, pleaded in vain for the pup's life, MacAlarney had lifted the little animal by the scruff of the neck and tossed it overboard.

The case was closed. The final report read "Accidental death at sea."

Most of the lieutenant's days were spent reading, lying on the sunny deck with his dog stretched out alongside.

Dave walked Kelly regularly, the end of the leash in one hand and a wad of newspaper in the other. Nobody seemed to mind the yellow stains the dog left behind; the other detail was quickly rolled up in the paper and dropped over the side.

One evening, thirty-two days out from the United States of America, Dave and Kelly stood at the prow of the ship watching the port of Bombay come in off the horizon. No one had been told that India was their destination but Dave recognized the Taj Mahal rising above the coastline like something out of the Arabian Nights.

They disembarked the third day after reaching port. Company B went over the side on a huge net to motor launches chugging in the morning sunlight. Before his descent, Dave roped Kelly under the armpits and lowered him to Jackson who had gone down ahead.

As they neared shore, Dave felt exhilarated and eager for what lay ahead. Kelly's front paws rested across the rail, his ears concentrating on the strange new sounds of the approaching dock. His black nose twitched at the unaccustomed odors and his eyes were glued to the throngs of milling people.

"Looks like we made it, my friend."

Dave slapped his dog affectionately across the shoulders. Kelly grinned and whined as his tail thumped against his master's leg.

From there on in, life moved swiftly. The 352nd was caught up in the machinery of war, like a wood chip in a raging torrent, and swept eastward with the tide past Rangapur, Chicardapur, and a hundred other strange names Dave could hardly pronounce.

The regiment crossed the Brahmaputra River into Assam, then rendezvoused in Ledo, five miles west of the Burma border.

The previous December, General Joe Stilwell, with two Chinese divisions, had crossed the watershed from Ledo into the jungles below the main mountain ranges. He had been opposed by the renowned Japanese Eighteenth Division but had forged ahead steadily and, by early January, had penetrated forty miles into Burma.

The 352nd rolled in behind, joining several other British and American engineer regiments already laboring in Vinegar Joe's wake, hacking a supply road out of a jungle that fought them as hard as the Japanese.

About a month after the arrival of the 352nd, Stilwell captured the airfield outside of Myitkyina by a swift advance of Merrill's Marauders. Reinforcements were flown in to assault the town, but the Japs held on obstinately until early August.

Kelly was there through it all. He and Dave got their first baptism of fire at Warzup at night, lying belly down in a slit trench while overhead the heavens trembled with Japanese aircraft and the air shrieked with the pain of slicing fragments of steel.

Kelly was there as strafing planes came in low over the treetops faster than the speed of sound—no one hearing them or seeing them until the tracers screamed down upon the toiling men.

Kelly learned fast, faster than the soldiers did. So they kept half an eye on him as they worked, and moved when he moved. But he also gave these men something else. His presence sparked a special brand of security. He was the dog back home, trotting aimlessly down a country road, confident in himself, completely unconcerned with the presence of death or

tomorrow. His indomitable spirit reached out and encompassed all, making better men of each and every one of them.

One in every ten of the G.I.'s harbored pets of some sort—cats, dogs, varieties of monkeys, lizards, chickens, goats, and even snakes. The men called them good luck charms—mascots—and other outfits nicknamed the regiment the "352nd Barnum and Bailey Show." But whatever the name, whatever the jokes, these animals filled a need. They were stabilizing factors in an unstable world. Love and affection were lavished upon them with a desperation that surpassed reason—with a hunger unfulfilled.

One evening Dave and Sergeant Jackson captured an enormous lizard that had gotten itself trapped in a culvert. It seemed harmless enough—narrow reptile head, long powerful tail, and all thirty pounds wrapped in a loose-fitting leather hide. They tied up the creature and dropped it in the back of the jeep. Here was a prize for someone special.

"Give him to Captain Rhome!" chuckled Condrasky. "The poor harassed son of a gun needs diversion—something to take his mind off himself and the company. Someone to talk to—someone to love!"

That sounded like a great idea.

Before daybreak, Dave fashioned a dog collar from a canvas belt and tied the monster to the captain's desk in the headquarters tent.

After chow, Dave and Condrasky, from the safety of a shell-torn tree trunk, watched Captain Rhome enter the canvas shelter. For one whole minute, by Dave's stopwatch, nothing happened. Maybe Rhome had dropped dead at the sight of the creature. Maybe— and then the roof caved in! *Whoosh!* The tent went mad, pulling its stakes loose. Rhome exploded into the open as if shot out of a gun, bellowing like a yellow-jacked steer. The giant lizard was clamped to his pants leg, and the table was still hooked to the lizard. In the air blast that followed came a hurricane of paperwork.

Kelly appeared out of nowhere and bore in, attacking the lizard from four directions at once. The reptile let go of the captain's trousers and, with the speed of a striking cobra, locked its powerful jaws on Kelly's tail.

When the smoke cleared, Kelly's broken appendage was in a splint and the lizard was back in the jungle where it belonged. It took almost three weeks for Kelly's tail to come out of hibernation and just about that long for Dave and Condrasky to emerge from the "doghouse."

Within the next month, Myitkyina fell, then Bahmo —and the convoys began rolling from Ledo to Kunming, China. In April of 1945, the 352nd Regiment was split up along the Ledo road with headquarters company based in Myitkyina. Company B bivouacked six miles from the western border, maintaining a twenty-mile stretch, continuously fighting back the jungle which pushed in from both sides like a green wall, striving to squeeze them out and take over. But the road was kept open and that twenty-mile strip became Company B's prison.

The rotation plan went into effect. Furloughs and leaves were granted to Karachi and Bombay and the good old U.S.A. Dave was promoted to First Lieutenant, but boredom weighed so heavily on his shoulders that he was unable to work up enough enthusiasm to celebrate.

The monsoons arrived early that year. It rained every day but, between the downpours, the sun came out, causing the jungle to steam like a Turkish bath in 103-degree heat.

The Irrawaddy River ran close to the bivouac area and in the late afternoons some of the men would go down for a quick dip. They had to stick close to shore because the river was at flood stage.

Dave lay on the river bank early one evening reading a book. Kelly sat beside him, watching Captain Fannin and Sergeant Jackson tossing a white tennis ball around. The men were standing knee deep in the shallows, but just beyond them the swirling brown water rushed southward, carrying with it uprooted trees and a wide assortment of other jungle vegetation.

The atmosphere was completely still, broken only by the voices of the two men. Suddenly Dave became aware of the doctor's shouting.

"No, Kelly! No! No!"

The white ball had been accidentally thrown out too far, and like a flash Kelly was after it. Even as Dave leaped to his feet, he saw Kelly reach the ball. The next instant the dog, with the white ball in his mouth, was whipped out into the powerful current. He was instantly sucked into a whirlpool, but surfaced thirty feet downstream. He must have known he was in trouble for he let the white ball go as he turned toward shore, swimming for his life.

Even as Dave plunged in after Kelly, a heavy branch rose up out of the depths like some prehistoric monster and got between them. But Dave was a powerful swimmer. He twisted to the left as the tree limb went by, then cut right again. For an instant he lost sight of the black dog but picked him out again a heartbeat later, frantically trying to board a swirling mass of vegetation.

Dave drove toward him with long powerful strokes. He caught up just as Kelly slid away from the greenery. His hand latched into the loose skin between the dog's shoulder blades, and he began pulling his way back to the shore, which was rushing past at an alarming rate of speed.

By this time, the bivouac area was out of sight. From the many aerial maps Dave had studied, he knew the river twisted its way through unchartered jungle. He swung his swimming arm over a passing tree trunk, hooking the other around Kelly just behind his forelegs. Dave stayed with the tree trunk for a bit, but let go when he noticed an enormous spotted snake coiled up beside him.

Slowly he worked his way out of the current, maneuvering his body carefully to avoid the frequent tangles of greenwood and foliage. By the time the man and dog reached shore, the tropical twilight had deepened considerably. The dense wall of the jungle hung over the shoreline, an impenetrable barricade that challenged anyone to break through.

All Dave had been wearing when he went to Kelly's rescue was khaki shorts. Now, as he stood in the water naked to his waist, the mosquitoes came down like a million pursuit planes to attack his unprotected body.

Kelly crouched beside him snapping frantically as the buzzing pests engulfed them. Dave figured that they were at least three miles below the camp. It was no great distance on a road, but through the massive jungle the going would be impossible. The only alternative was back the way they had come, through the shallow water with the shoreline as their guide.

Darkness had fallen and the night sounds began. Strange eerie birdcalls pierced the silence. The jungle seemed to come alive. It groaned and creaked and dripped as it grew, reaching out relentlessly in all directions like some giant octopus.

Dave had faced fear as a soldier in combat against known forces. But here alone with Kelly in the forest, he was gripped by a creeping terror the like of which he had never known. He and the dog stayed awake all night, huddled together against the bank. Dave's body was raw and numb from the constant onslaught of flying creatures. Kelly hunched miserably beside him.

Before dawn Dave fashioned a harness and leash from low-hanging vines. He fixed the harness to the dog's shoulders and attached the leash to his own waist. In this way he could prevent Kelly from being swept down river and also keep his hands free to pull them both upstream.

It was slow going. The protruding growth offered considerable help but the river bottom was knee deep in slimy mud. Just below the surface of the murky water, Dave could sometimes see long ribbon-like creatures that caused his skin to crawl as they slithered by.

At midday, the lieutenant and the dog climbed up on a high bank to remove the purple blood-sucking leeches from their bodies. The revolting creatures made Dave retch as he tore them loose from his bruised flesh. Kelly used his teeth.

Most of the time the water barely reached Dave's hips, but when it got deeper he helped the dog by lifting up on the harness. The sleepless night and the remorseless drag of the current finally drained away their strength. They stopped frequently to catch their wind, then pushed on, moving more and more slowly.

Shortly before sunset, Dave recognized the shoreline of the bivouac area. He called out for help and Kelly joined in as best he could. As they staggered up the bank, Captain Fannin and three others came running down to meet them.

The doctor eased Dave down on a cot in the hospital tent. He gave both the man and the dog an innoculation against infection and rubbed a soothing white ointment over Dave's mosquito-bitten back. Man and

dog were sound asleep before he finished.

When Dave awoke at noon the following day, Kelly was sitting beside him staring into his face. When the dog became aware that Dave's eyes were open, his ears flattened and his tail began thumping with joy as he pushed up against the cot.

Dave remembered the morning back at Van Dorn when he awakened to find that Kelly had recovered from the snake bite. His hand reached out to fondle the familiar black head he loved so much.

Three weeks later a request came from regimental headquarters: One officer and one noncom to head a convoy to Kunming, China. Dave, by now fully recovered from the river ordeal, frantically put in his bid and got the assignment. Sergeant Jackson was the noncom and Captain Fannin went along for the sights, riding with him in a command car at the tail end of the caravan. The drivers were Chinese and American soldiers, but Dave drove his own jeep up front with Kelly at his side.

The convoy pulled out of Ledo on a Tuesday morning in a heavy downpour. The road was slick but they made good time, bivouacking that evening two miles west of the Pangsaw pass. Dave was contented and happy to be on the move again.

They broke camp before daybreak and crossed the pass at dawn. The rain had stopped but the going was still tricky and treacherous. Almost two hours later, Dave's jeep was skidding down the eastward slope of the mountain with the thirty-truck convoy careening along behind.

Kelly's front paws were braced against the front dashboard but his eyes and ears were sharply alert, concentrating on the green tangle of jungle sliding by.

The lieutenant raised his hand to signal a rest break. Kelly, anticipating the halt, leaped from the still moving jeep. He was good at leaping from a moving vehicle. He could hit the ground, never missing a stride, then come aboard with the same split-hair timing. It was all part of his personality, first one in, first one out, and in their years together, Dave had never seen him make a mistake.

But today he did. Today, for two shocking seconds, Kelly was in the wrong place at the wrong time. The mud helped, and the spattered windshield, and a weapons carrier that came up behind and could not stop fast enough. It bounced the jeep off its front bumper and propelled it forward into a short, lopsided skid. Across the flat hood of the jeep, Kelly leaped into focus. Too late, Dave's boot struck the brake pedal, driving it down hard against the floorboard. The steering wheel spun uselessly in his hands while dog and jeep converged, then slammed together with a sickening jolt.

All sound seemed to cut out, as if the whole world had been struck dumb. Dave gripped the windshield frame and heaved himself out over the running board. As he cleared the front fender, Kelly was crawling toward him. The dog's eyes were on Dave's face but his forefeet clawed down into the mud, dragging the rest of him.

The lieutenant plowed in on his knees. With both

hands, he pressed into the thick ruff, gently easing the dog over on his side. He stripped off his field jacket, sliding it under the dog's head. Kelly began panting, but his eyes were still glued to Dave's face, watching his every move.

Sergeant Jackson came running up.

"You all right, Lieutenant?"

"Get Doc Fannin! Hurry!" Dave choked out. Something was constricting his throat.

Jackson wheeled without a word and ran back along the line of trucks. Before long, the doctor came slogging through the mud and hunched down over Kelly. Dave was unable to speak or move. His whole being was paralyzed by a single gripping fear that lay in his chest like a rock.

At last the doctor looked up. His eyes met Dave's for one brief instant before he climbed to his feet. He did not say a word. He didn't have to. His hand touched the lieutenant's shoulder as he turned away and walked slowly back to his vehicle.

Kelly whimpered softly. Dave remained where he was, staring down at his dog. A great weariness descended upon him, suffocating, choking him off from his surroundings. Then slowly he became aware that Sergeant Jackson was standing above him.

"Time to go, Lieutenant," the noncom said gently.

Without lifting his eyes, Dave answered, "Take the convoy on, Sergeant. I'll catch up."

The trucks crawled by, going downgrade, and the mist rolled in to fill the gap of their departure. In a little while Dave rose to his feet. He drew his .45 automatic from its holster. It felt cold and damp in his hand. He drew the lever back. As it snapped forward, the brass shell leaped up into the chamber.

The recoil of the pistol blast slammed against his

palm. The jungle magnified and re-echoed the flat, hard sound into a shattering barrage that rolled on up the valley, then died in the distance.

Dave walked back to the jeep and yanked a shovel from the rear compartment. The terrain rose and leveled off on his right. He scrambled to the top and began digging, but the network of vegetation and surface roots trapped the shovel. On hands and knees he attacked the earth, using the shovel like a spear, grasping huge hunks of sod with his hands, jerking them out, ripping, tearing.

When he finished, he reeled back to his dog and hung over him, dizzy with exhaustion. All he could hear was his pounding heart and sobbing breath. Then with great tenderness Dave wrapped his field coat around Kelly and carried him to the ragged hole. As the soaked earth fell in around the dog, covering him, the single silver bar pinned to the coat epaulet glowed for an instant in the fast fading light.

A sudden lonely terror swept over the man. With his combat knife, he slashed into a mottled tree truck that leaned over the mound of earth. With hacking, vicious strokes he carved "Lt. Kelly, 352 Engs."

Dave ran back to the jeep, dropped the shovel in the back seat, and climbed in behind the wheel. The motor roared and as the tires spun in the mud and took hold, he turned for one last look. But the grave was already swallowed up, forever lost in the jungle.

La Tour

LA TOUR WAS A tall chestnut gelding that lived for many years on Willow Farm in North Salem, a small village in upper Westchester County. His owner, John Watkins, had given him the name after viewing the Eiffel Tower in Paris on one of his many journeys abroad.

John Watkins rode the horse only about once a month. The rest of the time La Tour grazed over many acres of fertile pasture, along with a flock of sheep and a number of black Angus cattle. The red gelding was a handsome individual, a cross between coach horse and thoroughbred. He was a sweet, kindly fellow, calm and cool at all times—except when the Goldens Bridge Hunt passed Willow Farm.

This was La Tour's only opportunity to be in the company of other horses, and the big chestnut made the most of it. As the fox hunters jogged by, La Tour would race along the fence line, squealing and bucking as he went. When he reached the corner of the field, he would slide to a halt, swap ends, and repeat the maneuver again and again, following each group of riders, until the hunt was out of sight.

What was great sport to him was a downright nuisance to the mounted riders, many of whose horses began to blow up the moment the red horse arrived at the fence.

One crisp morning in the middle of October, La Tour was grazing peacefully in his meadow. He had been turned out early on this particular day and by ten o'clock had drifted toward the eastern side of his pasture.

Suddenly he lifted his head. There it was again, the unmistakable sound of the hunting horn. It came drifting up from the hollow beyond the woods that skirted the field. La Tour seemed to change from the quiet old farm horse into a magnificent charger. Head up, tail held high like a battle banner, he approached the fence and pulled up. He pranced as he waited, shaking his head impatiently.

He heard the hounds, then saw them briefly as they flashed through the woods, silent except for an occasional yelp of anticipation. The drum of hoofs came next, and soon, over the brow of a hill, the field appeared, galloping on, led by the master on a bay horse.

When the hunters thundered by his pasture, La Tour exploded into action. Head up and mane streaming, he galloped along the fence line, keeping abreast of them. But as he approached the corner of the pasture, he could see that the corner was no longer there. Sometime during the night an ancient maple tree had fallen and crushed the rail fence in its path.

La Tour checked his stride, but his blood was up. He shot through the opening and joined the hunt.

The field was moving downgrade. The red horse fell in behind. Nobody noticed his presence until one of the riders looked back and yelled, "Hey, look what we've got here!"

Somebody else called back, "That's Watkin's old horse. He must have jumped out!"

Only La Tour knew that he had not, because he actually had never jumped anything in his life—until half a minute later when he was confronted by his first stone wall.

The horses ahead took it in stride. La Tour came in too close but was lifted over by headlong momentum. He almost fell on his face on the far side but managed to recover and go on.

Some stragglers caught up and now the red horse found himself surrounded. Even if he had wished to pull out, it was too late. Hounds were running.

Someone cried, "Get that horse out of here!" But nobody was about to. The riders hit an open field and fanned out as they galloped across it. La Tour was getting into the spirit of things. He was free—he was on his own. The turf was blurring by as he flew over it. Nobody was paying much attention to him as they splashed through a brook and clambered up a steep grade. Mud and bits of flying stone pelted him as he struggled to keep up. Then another stone wall came at him and he scraped his knees as he went over. But the red horse was get-

ting the hang of it now—a crash course in jumping.

Abruptly the hounds went silent, and the field pulled up and checked briefly in a clearing. One of the whippers-in tried to drive the horse off, but La Tour was not about to go home yet. He dodged around the mounted man and cut back, just as the hounds opened up once more and away they went.

Within the next half hour La Tour jumped twelve stone walls. He fell over two more, but aside from a little lost skin was none the worse for it. But he was responsible for three other falls. He caused the first one when he stopped after a jump and the horse behind slammed into his big solid rump. The rider shot out of the saddle and landed right in the middle of La Tour's back. The man hung on for two seconds, then slid sideways and hit the ground rolling.

A moment later the red horse cut off another man in front of a stone wall, causing a three-horse pileup that delayed the hunt for nearly ten minutes.

"Get that troublemaker out of here before he kills someone!" screamed the master.

A man in a scarlet coat rode after La Tour with a hunting whip. The lash caught the red horse two sharp licks across the rump and he took off running, kicking up his heels as he went.

La Tour was getting tired of the chase, anyway. He really was not in condition for fox hunting. By now there was probably grain in his feedbox back home, but he wasn't sure how to get there. He came upon a narrow trail and turned into it.

Then, without warning, the hunt appeared up front, bearing right down on him. They had come around in a wide circle, and before the red horse could get out of the way, he was swept up and carried along with the tide of galloping horses.

The hounds were in full cry once again. There were heavy woods on both sides of the trail, and the only choice La Tour had was to keep going. He was really tired now. His coat was lathered white, and he was blowing hard—the only good thing about his predicament was that no one was riding him.

A huge stone wall came rushing up at him as he descended a long, rocky slope. He checked going into it, looking for a way out.

Whack! The sharp end of a hunting whip stung his rear end as someone yelled "Move it!" and La Tour jumped the wall out of pure shock. The land sloped off sharply on the far side, and the red horse stumbled downgrade for thirty yards before he could get his nose off the ground.

The hunt was running across some open fields. La Tour trailed along behind. His early exuberance had vanished and his legs, moving sluggishly beneath him, seemed filled with lead.

At last the hunters stopped to rest their horses, which had been running for almost two hours. The hounds had lost the fox. La Tour stood at the perimeter of the hunt, hanging his head. His sides were working like a huge bellows. He was absolutely exhausted —and thirsty.

118

When the hunt moved off once more, the red horse stayed where he was until they were all out of sight and his breathing came down to normal. Then he turned and began walking back the way he had come. He avoided the walls by worming his way through the woods, and though he did not know the country, some vague sense kept him moving in the general direction of home.

Before long he recognized the area he was in and quickened his step. At one point he stopped just long enough to rub his rump against the rough bark of a tree to relieve the smart of the welts left by the hunting whip.

Soon he sighted the red cattle shed above Willow Farm. Beyond that was the fence line. He followed along it until he came to the opening from which he had emerged only a couple of hours before.

He walked through it into his beautiful green pasture. At the brook that cut across one corner, he drank his fill, then played with the water, burying his muzzle in it and blowing bubbles.

From there he proceeded to his favorite dust bowl. He got down slowly and rolled in it for many minutes, grunting and groaning with ecstasy.

When he lunged to his feet, he shook himself until the dust hung above him like a golden halo.

It was good to be home again. He felt sore all over but hungry. His nose dropped down to the lush grass, and soon he was contentedly chomping away as if nothing unusual had happened.

Later that afternoon, Brent, the manager of Willow Farm, discovered the broken fence and repaired it.

When he reported to Mr. Watkins that evening he told him, "It was a lucky thing I spotted the break before La Tour did, or he would have gotten out for sure."

From that day on the chestnut horse never again ran

up and down the fence line when the hunt went by. He might watch the riders in a disinterested way, but most of the time he did not bother to lift his head from the serious business of grazing.

Perhaps in his own way La Tour had envied the hunt horses, galloping cross-country to the call of the hunting horn and the music of the hounds.

But he had tried it—and obviously had decided that it was not for him.

ABOUT THE AUTHOR-ILLUSTRATOR

SAM SAVITT and horses have been inseparable practically all of his life. He has written numerous books about horses in all fields, from rodeo to the Maryland Hunt Cup Race. His illustrations have appeared in *Sports Illustrated, True, Boys' Life,* and other national magazines, as well as in over ninety books. His drawings and paintings of horses have been recognized as some of the finest in the United States.

Pennsylvania-born Sam Savitt and his wife now live on a small farm in North Salem, New York. His favorite pastime—when away from his drawing board—is riding and schooling horses.